The
Parrot Who
Talked Too Much

Other books in this series:
The Cat Who Smelled Like Cabbage
The Dog Who Loved to Race
The Hamster Who Got Himself Stuck

Unless otherwise indicated, all Scripture references are from the Holy Bible: New International Version, copyright 1973, 1978, 1984 by the International Bible Society. Used by permission of Zondervan Bible Publishers.

Cover design by Durand Demlow
Illustrations by Anne Gavitt

THE PARROT WHO TALKED TOO MUCH
© 1990 by Neta Jackson
Published by Multnomah Press
10209 SE Division Street
Portland, Oregon 97266

Multnomah Press is a ministry of Multnomah School of the Bible, 8435 NE Glisan Street, Portland, Oregon 97220.

Printed in Singapore.

Library of Congress Cataloging-in-Publication Data

Jackson, Neta.
     The parrot who talked too much / Neta Jackson.
        p. cm. —(Pet parables)
      Summary: Jocko, a loud-mouthed parrot whose truthful comments often hurt the other animals in the pet shop, learns the importance of combining truth with tact and kindness. Includes a Bible verse and discussion questions
     ISBN 0-88070-415-2
     [1. Parrots—Fiction. 2. Animals—Fiction. 3. Conduct of life—Fiction 4. Parables.] I. Title. II Series: Jackson, Neta. Pet parables.
PZ7.J13684Par   1990
[E]—dc20
                                         90-48385
                                           CIP
                                         AC

91 92 93 94 95 96 97 98 99 - 10 9 8 7 6 5 4 3 2 1

The Parrot Who Talked Too Much

Neta Jackson

Illustrated by Anne Gavitt

MULTNOMAH

Portland, Oregon 97266

Jocko the Parrot opened one eye at the jingle of the bell. Ah-ha! Peter's Pet Shoppe was opening and a customer had just come in. Time to awaken the other animals.

"Good morning! Good morning!" Jocko screeched. "Wake up, sleepyheads. Awwk, sleepyheads!"

"Oh, shut up, Jocko," grumbled a deep voice below Jocko's cage. Old Dog was curled up in a worn dog bed on the floor and had no intention of getting up—not until Peter the Pet Shoppe Man dished out his breakfast, anyway.

"Good morning, Old Dog!" Jocko cackled. "Be alert! Look your best! Customers are coming! Ha, ha, ha." Jocko laughed at his little joke.

"Don't tease Old Dog," Mynah Bird piped up from her cage across the aisle. "You know he's Peter's pet and he's not for sale. Let him sleep."

"Yeah," grumbled Old Dog and closed his eyes again.

Jocko stretched first one claw, then the other, then bobbed his head up and down to get the crick out of his neck. "I feel mighty good this morning!" he squawked to no one in particular. The parrot cocked his head and looked in the mirror on the inside of his cage. "Looking mighty good this morning, too," he bragged.

It was true. Jocko had beautiful yellow and green feathers which shimmered in the sunlight. Red feathers decorated the curve of his wings, with a touch of blue toward the wing tips. His sharp eyes were bright red.

Jocko looked across the aisle at Mynah Bird's cage. "It's too bad you are so dark and plain, Mynah Bird," Jocko said, bobbing his head. "Don't you wish you had bright-colored feathers like I do?" Mynah Bird turned her back on Jocko and pretended not to hear. Peter the Pet Shoppe Man was calling for Old Dog.

"Breakfast time, Old Dog!" Jocko squawked. Old Dog got stiffly to his feet and waddled off down the aisle. "Don't eat too much, Fatty," Jocko called after him. "You're starting to get a little chubby around the middle."

"Be quiet, Jocko," scolded Mynah Bird. "You tease Old Dog too much."

"I'm not teasing him," Jocko sniffed. "I'm just telling the truth. He *is* getting fat and you know it."

The bell over the Pet Shoppe door jingled all morning; customers came in and out. Boys and girls who came by Jocko's cage exclaimed over his colorful feathers.

"Look at the pretty parrot, Mom!"

"Could we have a parrot, *please?* Huh? Please?"

"Listen to all the words he can say, Grandpa!"

Jocko bobbed his head up and down at all the attention and talked a blue streak. "What's up, Doc? . . . Always tell the truth! . . . What's for dinner? . . . Jocko wants pizza! . . . Answer the phone!"

Around noon Peter the Pet Shoppe Man put some fresh apples, seeds, and nuts in Jocko's cage. He was so busy eating that he didn't notice a new cage had been hung beside his until he heard a tiny warble. Jocko peered into the new cage. "Who are you?" he squawked to the little yellow bird.

"How do you do? I'm Canary!" chirped the yellow bird cheerfully.

"Hello, Canary," called Mynah Bird.

"Hello, Canary," Old Dog said from the floor.

"You sure are scrawny," Jocko noticed.

"Jocko! That's rude!" Mynah Bird scolded.

"Leave it to Jocko's big mouth," grumbled Old Dog.

"Don't get your tail in a knot," Jocko said. "I'm just telling it like it is. Look at her! She's scrawny!"

"Don't pay any attention to Jocko," Mynah Bird said to the new bird. "Welcome to Peter's Pet Shoppe, Canary."

"Thank you," chirped Canary. "This is my first pet shop. I'm so excited. I'm just learning to sing, too." And Canary warbled a little tune.

"You hit a wrong note," Jocko said.

Canary stopped singing.

Mynah Bird tried to change the subject. "The Pet Shoppe Man left your cage door open, Canary."

Canary brightened. "Oh, yes. I like to fly all over the shop. But I always come back to my cage."

And Canary hopped to her cage door, then darted into the air. She swooped around and around the Pet Shoppe before finally landing on the top of her cage. She was so excited she warbled a little song.

"Wrong note," Jocko commented.

The next day two children came in the Pet Shoppe to look at the birds. "Oh, look at the pretty little canary!" the little girl said. Canary chirped and whistled at her little mirror.

Jocko chuckled to himself. "They haven't seen anything yet!" he thought. He waited until they moved to his cage.

"What's the matter with the parrot's feathers?" asked the boy. "Mr. Peter!" he called. "What's wrong with the parrot?"

Wrong? Jocko looked in his mirror. His beak and head looked fine.

Peter the Pet Shoppe Man walked over to the bird cages. "Oh! Jocko the Parrot has started to molt," he said. "That's too bad. His pretty feathers will fall off for a while."

Jocko anxiously smoothed his chest with his beak. A big clump of green feathers came out and fell to the bottom of the cage. It was true! He was losing his pretty feathers! This was terrible!

The children patted Old Dog, then wandered away to look at the kittens.

Mynah Bird laughed. "Looks like you're losing your glory, Jocko!"

"Serves him right," mumbled Old Dog.

In the next few days, Jocko lost more and more feathers—even from the top of his head. "Hey, Baldy," snickered Old Dog. "You need a hat!"

"Quit calling me Baldy!" screeched Jocko.

"But, Jocko, we're just telling it like it is," Mynah Bird reminded him. And all the animals laughed.

Jocko knew it was true. He was bald and ugly. Big patches of skin showed where his feathers used to be. He couldn't bear to look in his mirror any more. He didn't feel like eating. He didn't feel like talking. He just sat in his cage and sulked.

Jocko used to like it when customers came by his cage. But now everybody said, "What's wrong with the bald parrot?" So Jocko just turned his back and didn't say anything.

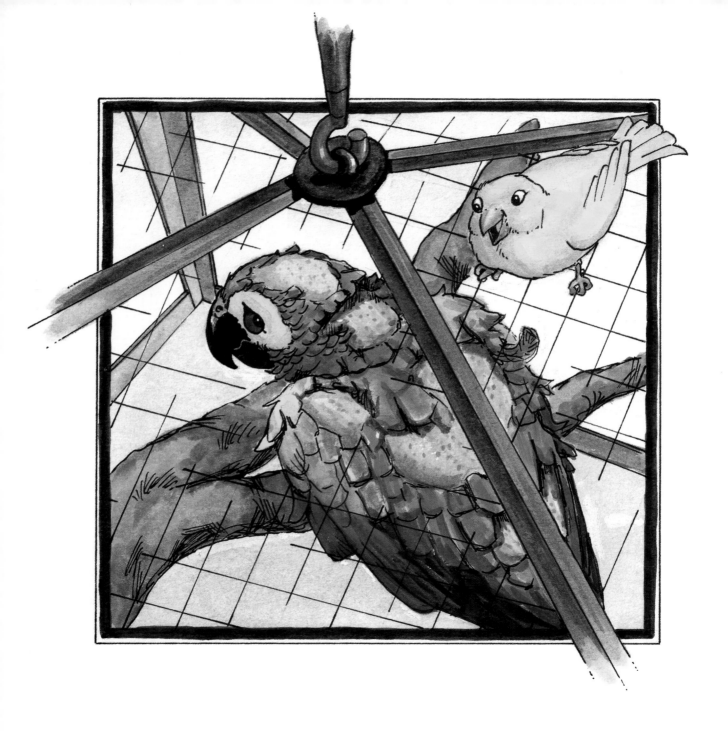

As Jocko sat in his cage feeling sorry for himself, Canary flew around the Pet Shoppe, then landed on top of Jocko's cage. She warbled happily. He was almost going to say, "Wrong note," but then remembered how ugly he looked, so he didn't say anything. Instead he listened. Canary's song *was* kind of pretty, even with the wrong notes.

"Good morning, Baldy!" called Mynah Bird when the bell over the door jingled in the morning.

"Feeling chilly, Baldy?" asked Old Dog as he waddled back to his bed after breakfast.

"Stop it, you two," scolded Canary. "You're just making Jocko feel worse than he already does."

It was true. Jocko felt very bad indeed. But Canary made him feel a little bit better. Jocko found himself looking forward to Canary's visits on the top of his cage. She would warble a song, and then chirp happily to him about all the comings and goings in the shop.

"You know, Jocko," she said, "you still have some pretty feathers. I like the red and blue ones along your wings." Jocko looked at his wings. It was true. He still had his red and blue feathers.

"And you have such a big nice cage."

Jocko looked around at his cage. It was a very nice cage.

"And I think you are very clever the way you can talk just like people! I like it when you say, 'Jocko wants pizza'!"

Jocko chuckled. That always made people laugh.

For a minute Jocko forgot that he was sulking. "You are very clever, too, Canary," Jocko said. "If you keep practicing, you will someday be a very great Song Bird."

"Oh, Jocko, do you really think so?" Canary was so happy she flew all around the Pet Shoppe twice.

Jocko watched Canary swoop back into her cage, and coo at her little mirror. Why, he had made Canary feel happy! It was a strange and wonderful feeling. Jocko ruffled his few remaining feathers and bobbed his head up and down.

It felt good to have a friend! It felt better than saying whatever he wanted to say—even if it was "true." Maybe the other animals would be his friends, too, if he looked for things to say that were true but didn't hurt their feelings.

Jocko decided to try again.

"Say, Mynah Bird," he called out. "Your black feathers look very shiny today!"

Mynah Bird tilted her head in surprise. "Why . . . thank you, Jocko!" She stretched out both wings to catch the sunlight and hopped gaily onto the swing at the top of her cage. "It's nice to hear you talking again."

Jocko blinked. It was working! Now, what could he find nice to say to Fatty . . . oops, he meant Old Dog.

"Instead, speaking the truth in love, we will in all things grow up into Him who is the Head, that is, Christ. From him the whole body . . . builds itself up in love . . ."
(Ephesians 4:15-16).

To the Parents

"But he hasn't got any clothes on!" exclaimed the boy as the Emperor paraded by. The truth was out—even though the Emperor was mortified and realized he'd been hoodwinked by his tailors. So goes the favorite fairy tale about "telling it like it is."

Kids are notoriously blunt about saying what they think or feel at any given moment—regardless of the social propriety. "Out of the mouth of babes" is a biblical reference to children speaking the simple truth even when adults can't see it. This is often a positive attribute and should not be unnecessarily squelched.

The other side of this attribute, however, is that children often speak "the truth" in a way that hurts others. This may happen innocently at first; but unfortunately many children quickly learn to use certain facts to tease, put down, or be unkind to someone else.

After reading the story of Jocko aloud to your child, you may want to use the following questions to discuss the difference between "telling it like it is" and speaking the truth in ways that are kind and loving.

1. What was Jocko's opinion about himself?

2. How did Mynah Bird feel when Jocko compared her black feathers with his bright-colored ones?

3. What did Jocko say to Old Dog that made him feel badly?

4. Did Jocko tell the truth when he told Canary that she hit a wrong note? Why did Canary stop singing?

5. What happened that changed Jocko's opinion of himself?

6. What did the other animals in the Pet Shoppe say to Jocko now? Were the things they said about Jocko true? How did they make Jocko feel?

7. What kinds of things did Canary do and say that helped cheer up Jocko?

8. Why did Jocko decide to change the way he talked to the other animals?

10. What do you think Jocko could say to Old Dog that was true but also kind?